The Pirate Ship

Gillian Cook

Illustrated by
Philip Bannister

Matador
9 Priory Business Park,
Wistow Road, Kibworth Beauchamp,
Leicestershire. LE8 0RX
Tel: 0116 279 2299
Email: books@troubador.co.uk
Web: www.troubador.co.uk/matador
Twitter: @matadorbooks

ISBN 978 1785899 270

British Library Cataloguing in Publication Data.
A catalogue record for this book is available from the British Library.

Typeset in 14pt Century Gothic by Troubador Publishing Ltd, Leicester, UK

Matador is an imprint of Troubador Publishing Ltd

To Cyrus and Cressida and all children who have loved and still love sailing the pirate ship in the hidden garden.

Corin and his sister, Carly, loved more than anything else to climb on the big pirate ship in an exciting hidden playground in London. They liked to climb all over it, going as high as they could up to the crow's nest and then going right down to the hold, where there was lots of sand. They always wished they could really sail the big pirate ship on water.

Corin would spend most of his time climbing the rope ladders, whereas Carly, who was six and one year younger than Corin, liked to try out everything else in the playground. After spending some time on the pirate ship she would make for the wooden 'listening post' where you can place your ear against the wire mesh and hear the magical, exciting sounds of the sea shore. It was just like holding one of those big shells against your ear and hearing the sound of the waves crashing on the beach.

While her brother tired himself out on the pirate ship and then on the slides, Carly would listen to the sea and then perch on some 'moving circles' going round and round before usually ending up on the swings.

One afternoon while their mother patiently waited, she was horrified to discover that Corin seemed to have disappeared. Her eyes had been anxiously scanning the busy play area, looking for both of her own children, but while she could see Carly by the listening post there was no sign of Corin. After running frantically all over the garden with Carly looking for him, she finally went to the big gates to get help from the gate keepers.

'My children have promised never to go out of the playground without me,' she told them, 'but I can't find Corin anywhere.'

'Don't you worry,' said the gate keeper kindly, 'parents often think their children have gone out of the playground, but they could never get past us. They are often afraid that their children might follow other families out and escape that way.'

'That's right,' said the other guard, 'though they could never get past us.'

Corin's mother turned away. She was a little reassured.

Meanwhile, Corin with his usual energy had tried out most of the things in the playground and had finally ended up in one of the little wooden houses on stilts. He was getting very, very tired and finally sat down feeling really exhausted. He was rather pleased to have the house all to himself to make a plan of action. Then, all of a sudden, he thought what fun it would be to go out of the gate and explore the park.

He saw a group of children were going out of the gate with three grown-ups and decided to follow the next group out.

It seemed really easy. Nobody seemed to notice.

Once outside he thought he would like to go to the Round Pond to see if there were any children sailing small boats on the water, but first he decided to explore his two favourite enormous statues in the park and so he made a beeline for the statue of a man on a horse. He loved to stand staring up at the huge rearing horse and its rider, who always looked as if he were about to fall off, although Corin could see that he really had a pretty good grip on the horse's reins. *There are lots of these huge statues all over London*, he thought. *There is even that extraordinary one of a man sitting in an armchair in the middle of Paddington station!*

As he stood there, Corin suddenly realised that two golden retriever dogs were watching him from a distance. When the dogs realised he had seen them, they turned and disappeared into the bushes.

After he had got tired of straining his neck to look at the horse and its rider, Corin started off in the direction of his other great favourite – the shining golden statue of a prince.

As he began to walk, he heard a great thundering of hooves and a frightening snorting sound behind him. He turned around in absolute terror but could see nothing. The horse and rider were exactly as he had left them. They obviously had not moved.

Corin thought he must have imagined it so he shrugged and then continued towards the other statue, which was a shining golden figure of a prince seated on his magnificent throne.

He ran down the long gravel path and then stood staring at the figure

...he heard a great thundering of hooves and a frightening snorting sound behind him.

seated high above him. As he gazed an extraordinary thing happened; the prince and his throne slowly revolved to face him and – even more extraordinarily – the prince gave him a friendly grin and an equally friendly wink. Corin felt rather awkward; he was not sure whether it was right to wink back at a grown-up, added to which he had never practised winking and was not sure how it would turn out. It might not look too cool. He decided to smile politely, which was just as well since there was no time for more as the prince and his throne revolved in a stately manner to their original position.

Corin wondered if he had been dreaming and stared and stared, but the prince was sitting as 'still as a statue' not flickering an eyelid and gazing with great interest at the large round building opposite.

The sun was shining on the amazing gilding and Corin said to himself, *I must have imagined it or perhaps the sun was in my eyes.*

Corin began to think that he had better get a move on to the Round Pond to look at the boats, but then thought he would just quickly explore another part of these lovely gardens where he remembered there were strange, mysterious little mounds and trees. Walking on, he saw ahead of him the same two golden retrievers who had been watching him earlier. He knew they were retrievers because his aunt and uncle had owned a retriever and he liked the way they trotted, swinging their hips and nodding their heads in a self-conscious way, as if they knew how beautiful they were. He walked towards them and asked if they were on their own.

'Oh yes,' said the bigger of the

two, 'we live in the park. I am Fluffles by the way, and this is my sister, Miss Muffy.'

'Don't you have anyone to look after you?' asked Corin.

'Oh no, we are very happy on our own,' said Miss Muffy. 'We lived with a family once but they did not take any notice of us and did not even see that the children were sometimes cruel to us. They never took us for a walk, not even at the weekend. Just once they employed a dog walker to take us out when they wanted to get us out of the way. Can you imagine it, dogs like us who are used to tearing round the countryside on our walks, having to walk so slowly in a row with three or four others, in a town of all places! It might suit some people. I know quite a lot of dogs who absolutely love it; they love the company and they love towns, but we felt so bored so we escaped just then and tore into

....he saw ahead of him the same two
golden retrievers who had
been watching him earlier.

the park and we have been here ever since.'

'But how do you get your food?' asked Corin, 'And where do you sleep?'

'Oh we have a very comfortable den deep in the bushes,' said Fluffles, 'and there is plenty of food around.'

'Yes, once we found an unopened packet of dog biscuits,' added Miss Muffy, 'not even out of date. Such nonsense to throw it away but it suited us very well. But really Fluffles, I am afraid we must get a move on and start looking for our supper tonight. By the way,' she said, 'why don't you sail the big pirate ship on the Round Pond?'

Corin looked puzzled. 'But I have just left the big pirate ship in the playground. How can it be on the Round Pond? Anyway, the water would not be deep enough. The ship is far too big.'

'I should just go and have a look,' said Miss Muffy. 'You could have such a lot of fun.'

'We will see you around then,' said Fluffles. 'Good luck.'

Corin felt sad to see them go and watched as they trotted off, neatly putting each paw one in front of the other, their long fluffy tails looking so elegant.

Corin decided that he ought to get on towards the Round Pond, but just then he saw a group in the distance and recognised some friends from his school: his best friend Ella, a Norwegian boy named Lars and a girl named Himali who was from Kathmandu. They seemed to be chatting to two pandas.

When he reached them Ella introduced the pandas as Pandemonium and Pandora. When Corin told them that his little sister had a toy panda that she was wild about,

Pandemonium laughed and said, 'She should come to the zoo and see us real ones. People go crazy about us. They just love us!'

He swung his arms against his chest and laughed happily. The pandas looked very cuddly but Corin could not help staring at their stained teeth. *Perhaps they don't get a chance to clean their teeth very often*, he thought, *or perhaps it is all those bamboo shoots they eat.*

The pandas had a whole pile of bamboo shoots in front of them and were constantly reaching out for them.

'Don't you get tired of eating the same thing all the time?' he asked.

'Oh no, we love bamboo,' said Pandora as she reached for another one, 'we can never get enough of it.'

'I wish we had pandas in Norway,' said Lars, 'but we have some lovely husky dogs. People say they are vicious, but it is only when they are fighting over their food. Two of our dogs, Inger and Gunnar, were very affectionate. Inger had lovely white fur and she was really tough, even stronger than Gunnar and he could pull most things. I really miss having a cuddle with them.'

'We ought to be getting back now,' sighed Pandora. 'Our poor old keeper, Freddie, will be cutting capers! He is very sweet though really and turns a blind eye to all our little escapades. He knows all about our secret tunnel from the zoo to this place but as long as we are back by visiting time to see the children he does not seem to mind. The children want to see us; they make a great fuss of us.'

'Yes,' agreed Pandemonium, 'and we love to see them too and we don't want to disappoint them, so we really ought to go now, but we just had to come and see our old friend Ella here. We often meet for a chat.'

'You never told me,' said Corin to Ella, suddenly feeling rather hurt.

'I couldn't, it was a secret. I promised the pandas. You cannot tell even your best friend absolutely everything.'

'That's quite true,' said Himali, 'Lars and I were just walking through the park and we just happened to bump into Ella with the pandas. She did not really want us to see them.'

'I suppose I had better take my nail varnish off now,' sighed Pandora, looking sadly at her nails, which she had painted dark blue. 'Freddie might say that the children will not like it.'

'I like it. I think it looks very pretty,' said Lars.

'So do I,' chorused the others.

'There you are,' laughed Pandemonium, 'these children like

it, so keep it on. You know you like a little flutter!

Why don't you sail the big pirate ship on the Round Pond?' he asked suddenly turning to Corin.

Corin stared in amazement. 'How extraordinary, that is just what Miss Muffy told me to do, but I have just left the pirate ship in the playground, so how can it be on the Round Pond? And the water would not be deep enough. Also I haven't brought my sailing boat.' He thought longingly of his small sailing boat sitting on the windowsill at home.

'You won't need it,' said Pandora. 'You will have the big pirate ship to sail. It is waiting for you. It is moored on the Round Pond. Why don't you just go and see. You would just love sailing it.'

The children found it very difficult to believe but said politely that they would go and find it.

...'I couldn't, it was a secret . I promised
the pandas. You cannot tell even your
best friends absolutely everything.'

They said goodbye to the pandas and set off. They had not gone very far into a rather deserted part of the park when they heard a great roar and there in the distance was a huge mastiff. It was baring its teeth, looking horribly angry and advancing at great speed.

'Stick close together,' said Ella, 'we can fight it.'

'I'm not afraid,' said Lars.

'Neither am I. Anyway there are four of us,' said Himali.

They were all terrified and shaking but tried not to show how frightened they were. They watched as the fierce animal got closer and closer. It had huge jaws and was snarling horribly.

'Make really frightening, snarling faces as well and terrible snarling noises. Clench your hands out like claws. Keep together and walk towards it. This all we can do' advised Corin.

Just as the mastiff got to within thirty feet of the children there was a flash of gold fur and two golden retrievers rushed out of the bushes and stood between the children and the mastiff.

When the fierce creature saw Fluffles and Miss Muffy looking so fiercely determined, it stopped immediately and started to shake and cower. Then it turned its back and tore off as fast as it could go and was soon lost in the distance.

The two dogs trotted up to the children looking pleased with themselves and wagging their long furry tails. Fluffles was even laughing.

'That saw him off,' he said, 'the great cowardly bully. Like all big bullies, he never goes for anyone his own size and always picks on someone smaller.'

'It is no laughing matter, Fluffles,' said Miss Muffy. 'That dog is a menace. We really will have to turn ourselves into vigilantes to protect all these children.'

The four friends threw their arms round Fluffles and Miss Muffy.

'But how did you know we were in danger?' asked Corin.

'We just had a feeling,' said Fluffles. 'That dog has been roaming around here lately and we started worrying about you.'

'Yes, it has become quite a business,' said Miss Muffy. 'We spend a lot of time retrieving small children and returning them to their parents.'

'Yes, perhaps we should turn it into a real business,' joked Fluffles. 'We could advertise:
"Retrievers Service – You lose 'em, we find 'em!"'

'Really Fluffles!' said his sister, pretending to be shocked but trying not to laugh. 'Anyway, we really must go and look for our supper now. We still have not found anything.'

'Sure thing! We'll see you around,' Fluffles told the friends cheerfully.

They all waved goodbye and the four friends continued through the park.

It was getting darker and darker as they got further into the wood and the trees and undergrowth became denser and denser, so that it gave them all a shock when a tall and extremely unkempt looking man suddenly stepped out of the bushes in front of them. He wore a long, brown, dirty overcoat to his ankles and had very muddy boots. His hair was very matted and his face with its long tangled beard was certainly most unfriendly and sinister looking. Corin noticed his dirty and torn shirt with a skull and cross-bones printed on it and he noticed what looked like a cutlass hanging down at the man's side underneath his long coat.

'Do you know the way to the Round Pond?' The stranger asked abruptly.

...'Do you know the way
to the Round Pond?'

'Well, we are just....' Ella was about to say 'Well we are just on our way there', but Corin stepped swiftly in front of her and addressed the man

'No, I am afraid we can't help you, we don't know the way', he lied.

Corin did not trust the man at all and had no intention of letting him accompany them.

'Where are you going then?' asked the man, 'what are kids like you doing here all on your own?'

'We might ask the same of you', replied Corin in his most grown-up manner.

A look of fury shot over the stranger's face. He took a menacing step towards Corin, and then thought better of it as the friends closed quickly round Corin. 'Not very friendly and polite are you?' he sneered,

'We are perfectly friendly and polite to people who are friendly and polite to us' answered Himali.

The man swung round In fury and looked about to hit her, but then thought better of it.

Lars put his arm around Himali, who started to look frightened. 'We must be on our way' he told the man. 'We are only out exploring the park at the moment. Our family is nearby with a picnic and we have got to go and join them'. He was rather pleased with himself for thinking up this piece of information on the spot.

The man looked hard at each of them in turn. 'Perhaps we will meet again' he said in sinister tones 'or maybe it will be my friends that you will meet if you do go to the Round Pond. They are always looking out for small children like you.'

'We are not small. We are all big' Corin replied furiously.

'My friends do a lot of sailing on the Round Pond' said the man with a sneer. 'It is their territory see'.

Corin looked astonished. 'What sort of sailing?' he couldn't help asking. He knew the men would not be sailing small boats and he knew the pond was quite small. He then remembered the words of the retrievers and pandas and what they had said about the pirate ship being moored there.

The stranger looked at him sullenly. 'You'll see' he said, 'You'll get what you deserve there.'

The children suddenly felt very frightened; everything seemed to be getting very nasty.

'We must get on now' said Corin 'We can't stand here talking all day, as Lars said – our family will be waiting for us.'

The man looked at them all carefully with his menacing leer. 'Don't trust those stupid retrievers and pandas if you bump into them. They are useless, they won't help you.'

'Oh yes they will,' said the children all together. 'They have already helped us' added Ella.

'I have wasted enough time here already just talking to stupid children' he snarled. Then he turned and strode off towards the bushes and disappeared as suddenly as he had come.

'Well, at last he has gone' said Ella shakily 'Let's get a move on now quickly in case he comes back.'

The weather had changed; it had suddenly got colder. The sun had gone behind the clouds, and when they finally got to the Round Pond there were no small sailing boats and no other children. The water looked cold and grey and ruffled and uninviting. Worst of all, there was no sign anywhere of the big pirate ship.

The children were very disappointed.

'I thought it was too good to be true,' said Corin sadly. 'I couldn't believe it would be there and yet the pandas and Miss Muffy seemed so sure. Would you mind waiting a bit longer just in case?' he asked the others.

'No, I would like to. The pandas are usually very reliable,' said Ella, 'I don't think they would raise our hopes for nothing.'

'Yes, we owe it to the pandas somehow, to wait a little longer,' said Himali.

'I don't mind waiting,' said Lars, 'I really think we ought to.'

'Also, Miss Muffy really seemed to promise that it would be here,' said Corin. 'Yes, we really ought to wait.'

THEN SUDDENLY IT WAS THERE. THE PIRATE SHIP WAS REALLY THERE ON THE WATER!

It was moored at the side of the Round Pond. The sun had come out and the sails shone white and fluttered in the breeze and seemed to be inviting them all on board.

The friends ran to the ship. They swung up the rope ladders and untied the mooring rope and the pirate ship sailed out on to the water. Strangely, the water seemed just deep enough for the big ship to sail on. It was now really hot, but there was enough wind to fill the sails.

Corin was just wishing he had brought his pirate suit with him, when to his astonishment he saw it on the locker beside him, together with the wonderful hat with the skull and cross-bones that he had been given for Christmas. He quickly put them on and saw that the others were also wearing pirate outfits.

To and fro they sailed in the sun from shore to shore and Corin felt he

...to and fro they sailed from shore
to shore and Corin felt
he had never been so happy.

had never been so happy. They did not see any other pirate ships, but they were really very glad. After the terrifying ordeal with the mastiff they certainly did not feel like fighting. They had quite enough to do now, and more than enough excitement managing the big ship. They all took it in turn to steer and pull on the ropes. It was quite hard work but they felt they were really in control of the ship.

Corin realised though that there was just one thing missing. *If only Carly were here*, he thought to himself, *she would just love this. We must bring her next time*, he decided. *She would soon learn the ropes and would be brilliant at sailing. After all, we both always wished we could really sail the big pirate ship on the water.*

They must have been out on the pond for about forty minutes when Corin began to feel guilty that his mother and sister might be worrying about him and thought perhaps that they ought to go back. Just at that moment, however, he saw a brown speck in the distance coming towards them. It was another pirate ship and it was even bigger than their own. As it drew nearer they could see a crew of very fierce looking men, all of them in very scruffy pirate clothes. They were flashing their swords in a terrifying way. They soon came alongside and two of them climbed aboard, grabbing Himali and Ella and tying their hands behind their own backs.

'Leave us alone!' shouted Himali, 'You are hurting my hands.'

'You will hurt a lot more where you are going. It will be hard labour for you,' said the pirate with a cruel laugh. 'As for you boys, it will be the same for you too, hard labour, in another place. Either that or you will walk the plank.'

'You won't get away with it!'

shouted Corin. 'Fluffles and Miss Muffy our golden retriever friends will get you. They have rescued us from worse thugs than you. That mastiff was far more frightening than you could ever be.'

One of the fiercest pirates gave Corin a hard cuff around the head.

'Are you talking about those pathetic dogs? All they did was phone the zoo. The bigger one got out his mobile phone and seemed to be talking to some panda. A fat lot of good that will do. Anyway they were already in a tizzy trying to find some children who had got lost in their park.'

'Oh that means Pandemonium will get the PPP out,' interrupted Ella. 'That's The Panda Police Patrol. They are very quick operators. The other day there was an incident at the zoo. A child poked a stick at Pandora and caused a slight bruise. Pandemonium was furious and so was Freddie. He told the child's mother off because she just watched as the child poked at Pandora, and did nothing to stop him. Anyway Freddie phoned the PPP and got them out and they told the mother that they would not be allowed to visit the zoo again.' Ella started to look much happier at the thought of Freddie's help and the help of the PPP.

'Shut up and stop the cackle,' said one of the pirates rudely.

They began to tie up Lars's hands. Lars then started to laugh and the pirates all looked startled and followed his gaze. In the distance was a motor launch making rapid progress towards them.

'It looks as if you are the ones who will be doing hard labour,' said Lars. He was laughing so much that Himali couldn't help but join in and was doubled up with laughter.

'Everyone has trusted the retrievers and the pandas and our trust has always been rewarded. They will rescue us again,' she said, bravely ignoring the furious look of the fierce pirate.

The pirates were clearly terrified. Everyone knew about the PPP.

By this time the launch had drawn up alongside them. The PPP was a very smart squad. They might not have been very quick on their feet but they were brilliant marksmen. Together with the Gorilla SAS they were a formidable team and every criminal feared them.

The Gorillas were close behind the PPP and as the PPP trained their guns on the pirates, the Gorillas moved swiftly in to handcuff them.

It was an amazing sight. The Panda Police Patrol in their smart navy uniform and peaked caps and the Gorilla SAS in their khaki uniform, towering over everyone, were all terrifying.

They soon had all the pirates handcuffed and herded into their launches.

'Can we escort you anywhere?' the officer in charge of the PPP asked Corin.

'No thank you,' said Corin, 'I think we will sail to the shore now. I feel a bit guilty. My mother and my little sister will be looking for me as I escaped from the secret playground and I didn't mean to be away for so long.'

The officer looked severely at Corin but obviously thought he had had enough shocks for one day and did not comment.

The two launches moved off and the four friends prepared to sail back.

'I can't wait to tell Carly all about this. We really must bring her next time,' said Corin, turning to his friends.

Just as he said her name, he heard

her voice. She was saying over and over again:

'I have found Corin, Mummy. He is up here in the stilt house. Climb up here and see. He is fast asleep.'

Then Corin woke up to find his mother and sister hugging him over and over again.

'I couldn't believe you would really go out of the playground,' said his mother, 'and the gate keepers said you wouldn't get past them! It is wonderful that we have found you safe and sound. What a relief! Now I think we should all go and celebrate. Let's find a nice cafe nearby and have a really special tea.'

'But it did really seem as if I went out of the playground,' said Corin. 'It was all so real. I met Fluffles and Miss Muffy, those two lovely retrievers who are always in the park. They are always on their own and they always look so busy as if they are on some sort of adventure – that is why I dreamt about them because I am always thinking about them.'

Then Corin proceeded to tell his mother and his sister all about his dream.

Carly said that she had also noticed the two beautiful dogs several times and had often thought of going up to them, but she had also noticed that they always seemed to be in a hurry. Once she had been on her scooter and had tried to follow them but they had seemed to be very quick and had soon disappeared.

Their mother was worried about the retrievers hunting for their food and being out in all weathers in the park and said that she thought that perhaps they ought to ask them to come and live with them. 'They sound such lovely dogs' she said. 'It would be such fun to have them and we would certainly take them for nice walks.'

Corin looked doubtful however and pointed out that they had told him that they loved the outdoor life and that they seemed to have no difficulty in getting food. Also it seemed as if Fluffles and Miss Muffy felt that they had a duty to look after all the children who got lost or got into trouble in the park.

Carly had the last word though:

'I have an idea. Let's get Lars and Himali and Ella together and get them to come to the park next Saturday with us. They always love a trip to the park and they love the pirate ship. This time though I am really going to go up to those dogs and I am going to say Hello Fluffles. Hello Miss Muffy. Would you like to come and visit the pirate ship with us and would you also like to come and live with us?"'

Lightning Source UK Ltd.
Milton Keynes UK
UKHW02f0652010318
318679UK00005B/279/P

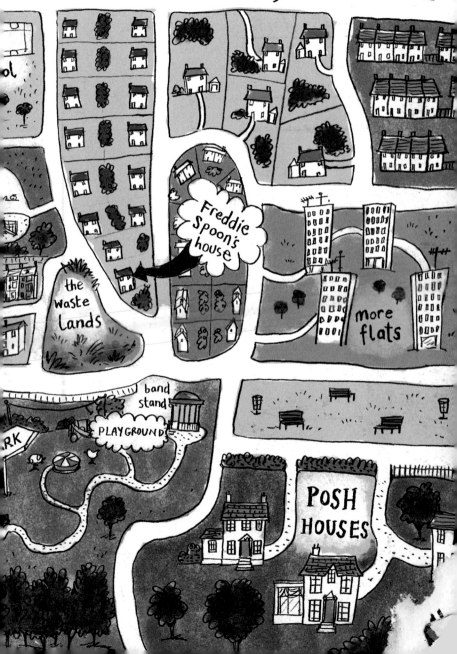

For Kat, with love. Mum x
C. H.

For Martha and Fred
S. W.

First published in the UK in 2017 by Nosy Crow Ltd
The Crow's Nest, 14 Baden Place, Crosby Row,
London, SE1 1YW, UK

Nosy Crow and associated logos are trademarks and/or registered
trademarks of Nosy Crow Ltd

A CIP catalogue record for this book will be available from the British Library.

Printed and bound in Turkey by Imago

Papers used by Nosy Crow are made from wood grown in
sustainable forests.

ISBN: 978 0 85763 915 8

www.nosycrow.com

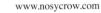

The BEAST of BRAMBLE WOODS

My dad says that if you want something badly enough, you'll get it. You just have to work hard. I worked hard for my spelling test last week and got 7 out of 10, which I thought was pretty good, especially as one of the words I got right was parrashoot…

Chapter One
Pester Power

My friend Freddie Spoon says that if you want something from your mum or dad, you have to work really hard to persuade them. It's called Pester Power and here's how you do it:

1. Wait till your chosen parent is looking relaxed and not busy.

2. Make them a cup of tea with
   two sugars and a biscuit.

3. Ask them if they've
   had a nice day.

4. Tell them how good you've been.

5. Tilt your head to one side and look up at your parent with big sad eyes.

6. Ask for the
   thing you want.
   Remember to say
   "Pleeeeeaaassssse."

7. If they say no, repeat steps
   1 to 6. Around 500 times
   should do it.

If they still say no or get cross,
ask the other parent.

Freddie Spoon says it works a treat.
I once managed to get as far as Step
4, but then I heard snoring and
realised my dad was actually
asleep, with his eyes
closed.

So there wasn't much point doing the
tilty head and big eyes thing. And Mum is

always busy with us kids and Granny and
the Baby so there's no point even trying
Pester Power on her.

Chapter Two
The Perfect Mix

By the way, I'm Nell. Well, that's my nickname. My real name is Antonella Henry.

Some boys are actually called Henry for their first name. It's a good job I'm not a boy or I might have been called Henry Henry, which would have been very silly and quite embarrassing.

Luckily, I'm a girl, and my dad says I'm the Perfect Mix because I have brown eyes and curly hair like him, and a little nose and wide smile like my mum. That's why they decided to call me Antonella, because it's a mixture of their names.

Anthony and Isabella.

Anton-ella.

See?

I don't look much like Lucas, thank goodness. He's my Big Brother and he's as pale as pale and his hair is all straight and floppy. My mum says it's because his *birth* daddy has blond hair and pale skin. I think it's because he stays in bed all day and never gets any sun. He does this because he's a teenager. Mum says teenagers need a lot of sleep because their brains turn to mush, which makes everything twice as hard.

I said, "Also, doing homework until three o'clock in the morning must be pretty tiring."

Lucas had done a LOT of stomping around that night. I think his homework must have been especially tricky.

Chapter Three
Snakes and Panthers

So the other day, me and Freddie Spoon were in our den in Mrs Next Door's garden, playing with Mr Fluffy. Freddie Spoon says Mr Fluffy is nearly a World Record Holder. He says a lady in a suit came to Mrs Next Door's house once with a purr-ometer. He says Mr Fluffy is the second-loudest purrer in the whole country! First loudest is a black-and-white cat in Torquay called Merlin.

I said, "Why doesn't Mr Fluffy ever purr when *I'm* around?"

Freddie Spoon just shrugged. "Dunno," he said. "Look at this." He showed me a piece of torn-out newspaper. On it was a fuzzy photo of a big black splodge. This is what it looked like:

MYSTERIOUS BEAST CAPTURED ON FILM

A mysterious beast has been captured on film by local photographer, Ms Barking.

Ms Barking said, "I saw this mysterious beast at the bottom of my garden, so I took this photograph." When asked what she thought the animal was, Ms Barking replied, "It's a mystery."

"I know," said Joe. "Let's tell ghost stories!"

Lucas said he'd start, so we all sat down on the rugs. Lucas put on a spooky voice and said, "It was a dark, dark night…"

I got up and stood really close and Lucas shouted, "Hey! That's cheating!" He tried to grab me, so I pulled the sausage off the pole and threw it over the fence.

MS Barking

Freddie Spoon said, "I reckon
it's a panther. Panthers are always
escaping from zoos and places."

I said wasn't it a bit cold and rainy for panthers, but Freddie Spoon said they've evolved and adapted and grown thicker fur so they can survive. Me and Freddie Spoon know a lot about wildlife because we're going to be wildlife experts when we grow up.

He said we should break into the zoo one night and let all the animals out. "Imagine the carnage!" he said. "The lions would rampage around stealing babies and chomping postmen. And the buffalos and zebras would run riot up and down the streets bashing up all the cars and making traffic jams!"

21

"And," I said, "the snakes would slither down the drainpipes and come up in people's toilets and see a delicious peach, and take a bite, only it wouldn't be a peach it would be someone's bottom!"

Freddie Spoon told me not to be stupid. He said, "Snakes don't eat peaches." Which made it even funnier and we fell about laughing until it was time for tea.

23

Chapter Four
Pester Power Part Two

Inside, the house was in chaos. This was nothing new, our house is always in chaos, but this was different to the usual thing. The kitchen was full of bags and boxes and sleeping bags and also two boys called William and Joe, who are Lucas's nerdy friends.

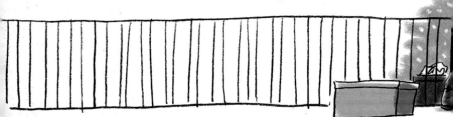

25

When I asked what was going on, Lucas said, "We're camping out to celebrate the end of exams."

A camp out? Great!

I said, "Where are we going
to sleep? Are we going to have a
campfire? Can we stay up late?"

But Lucas said, "*You* can't come!
It's just me and the boys!"

I said, "What? Why? We want
to camp out too, don't we, Freddie
Spoon?"

William and Joe shuffled about,
awkwardly. Lucas put on his
annoying teasing voice and said,
"Poor Nelly-kins, you're much too
wickle to camp out in the wild.

"You might get scared of the dark. You might throw yourself into the fire and get frazzled. You might get eaten by a nasty scary bear!"

28

I shouted,

"MUM!
THAT IS
SO UNFAIR!
WE WANT
TO CAMP
OUT TOO!
MAKE HIM
LET US!"

Mum said, "No, darling. It's Lucas's special time. You and Freddie can watch a movie with Daddy and me."

I. WAS. FUMING!

I knew I should deploy the Pester
Power plan, but there was no time,
so I skipped straight to Step 5. I did
the tilty head thing and made my
eyes all big. "Pleeeeaaassse!"

But then the phone rang and Mum jumped up from her sewing machine to answer it and got tangled up in bunting and nearly tripped over and then the Baby started wailing and I knew I wasn't going to get anywhere. So I made a cup of tea and went to find Dad.

"Hi Daddy," I said. "How was your day?"

Dad was watching football. "Fine thanks, love. How was yours?"

I told him I'd got a gold star for good work, which was not actually true, but desperate times need desperate measures. I sat on his knee for a cuddle, and also so he couldn't see the telly. Then I made big eyes and tilted my head to one side. "Daddeeee?"

"Yes, Nell?"

"You know Lucas is camping out tonight with his friends? Well, please can me and Freddie join in? We'll be ever so good and..."

But Dad said, "No, love. Not tonight," and he tried to look round me at the TV.

So I moved my head again and said, "But Daddy, we won't be any trouble and it would be really good for our education."

Dad shuffled me to one side, staring at the screen. "Well maybe … just … wait…"

So I got in the way again and said, "So *can* we?"

And Dad groaned, "Yes, yes, whatever, but make sure you're back in the house by eight-thirty."

EIGHT THIRTY!!! "But Dad...!" I said.
Suddenly there was a roar from the TV
and Dad jumped up, nearly knocking me
to the floor.

"Gooooalll!"

And that was that.

Chapter Five
It was a dark, dark night...

Lucas was not happy. "It's not fair! Babysitting two *children* is going to ruin our Epic Night Out!"

Mum was not happy because Dad had gone and said yes after she'd said no. But she couldn't say anything because of Parent Solidarity. Parent Solidarity is when your mum and dad pretend to agree, even when they don't agree at all. It's because they want you to think all their decisions are FINAL. It's their only real weapon against Pester Power.

I was not happy either. "It's *worse* for us! You get to stay out *all* night and we have to go inside at stupid eight thirty!"

Then Freddie Spoon tugged my sleeve and whispered, "Just because we have to GO inside, it doesn't mean we have to STAY there!"

I said, "Oh Em Gee! Freddie Spoon, you are a genius!!"

We helped put the tents up and lay out some rugs, then Dad came out to light a campfire in a special metal bucket thing. Mum brought out some sausages on a tray and we put them on sticks and roasted them over the fire. It was so fun!

Lucas's first sausage fell right into the fire and when he finally managed to fish it out it was burnt to a smithereen and he had to start again with a new one. Freddie Spoon skewered the burnt sausage on to the top of the tent pole! He said, "The Sausage of Doom is watching over you!" We all fell

about laughing. Except Lucas. He was still cross. Then William and Joe tried to turn their laughs into coughs which was even funnier and in the end we were all laughing together.

Then, one of the boys threw a peanut at
the Sausage of Doom and hit it first time!
"Last one to hit the Sausage of Doom has
to eat it!" Freddie Spoon shouted.

So we all grabbed handfuls of peanuts
and started firing.

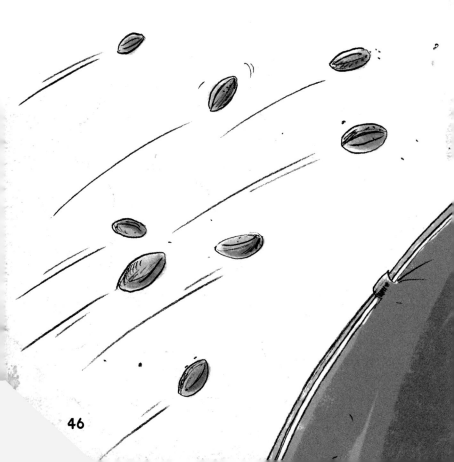

But Freddie Spoon interrupted. "Oh that's so corny. I've got a much better story and it's actually true." He told them about the Mysterious Beast. He said that it was spotted really nearby and that it was breaking into people's houses and stealing their babies out of their cots and biting postmen. Lucas and his nerdy friends groaned and laughed and said what a load of rubbish. But Freddie Spoon didn't care. He showed them the newspaper cutting and said, "You mark my words, that Beast is out there and it's coming for YOU!"

Lucas and his nerdy friends looked at each other then Dad shouted from the back door, "Nell, Freddie, time to come in!"

As we stood up, Lucas grinned meanly. "Night-night, babies. Don't forget your dummies!"

Chapter Six
Dares

We said goodnight to Mum and Dad. My dad asked if we wanted a story, but I did a fake yawn and stretch. I said, "No thanks, we're both *really* tired." Dad looked a bit surprised, then shrugged. "Oh. OK then. Night."

Upstairs, we stuffed our pillows under the covers to make it look like we were in bed. Then we put on woolly hats so that Lucas and his nerdy friends wouldn't spot us. Then we hid on the landing to wait.

Soon enough, Mum came up with the

Baby. She poked
her head around my
door and whispered,
"Goodnight, you
two." Freddie Spoon
started giggling so I
clamped my hand
over his mouth to
stop him making a
noise, and his giggle
came out of his nose
and on to my hand.
Euuuk!

When Mum went into her room, me and Freddie Spoon crept down the stairs and sneaked out of the back door. We used special hand signals to communicate as we crawled through the fence into Mrs Next Door's garden. Then we hunkered down to spy on the boys.

They were still sitting round, poking the fire with sticks and waving them around making patterns with the glowing ends. Freddie Spoon whispered to me, "Dare you to go and steal their marshmallows."

I gaped at him. "But they'll see me!" I said.

"Not if you're super-silent and super-careful," Freddie Spoon said. So I squeezed back through the fence and stealth-crawled on my elbows towards the camp.

Carefully I sneaked round the side of the tent and pulled the marshmallows

from a box. The
packet made a loud
crinkling sound but the
boys were busy trying
to get sticks to build
a bonfire, so luckily
they were distracted.

I rushed back to our hiding place, giggling uncontrollably. Then me and Freddie Spoon dived into our den and played Chubby Bunny. Have you ever played it? It's so fun. You stuff as many marshmallows as you can into your mouth and try to say,

"Chubby Bunny."

The person who laughs first is the loser. We both lost straight away but that's how the game goes.

Suddenly I heard a shout. "Hey! Where's

the marshmallows?" I peeped through the fence to watch as Lucas pulled everything out of the box, searching. But of course he didn't find them! "We can't have a bonfire without marshmallows!" he groaned.

Then William – or it might have been

Joe – said, "Maybe the Beast of Bramble Woods crept in and took them!"

Lucas laughed. "Ha ha! Yeah, right…" But his eyes flicked nervously towards the woods on the other side of the fence.

Chapter Seven
Caught

Back in our den, Freddie Spoon picked his
pet frog out of its tank and tried to feed
it a marshmallow. I don't think frogs like
marshmallows because it just sat there,
looking bored. I said, "Dare you to put him
in their tent."

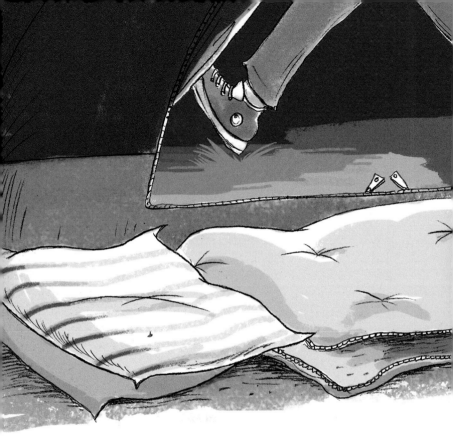

Freddie Spoon was out and back in a flash, looking red and puffed out and grinning like an idiot.

A few minutes later one of the boys went in to find a torch, and ran out yelling, "There's something moving in my sleeping bag!"

Me and Freddie Spoon rolled around laughing. "This is the Best Fun EVER!" I snorted.

Freddie Spoon dared me to pull the tent pegs out, and I nearly got away with it, but as I was escaping, I tripped over one of the guy ropes and Lucas grabbed me!

"GOT YOU!" he cried. "I'm telling Mum and you're going to be in SO much trouble."

I struggled hard and shouted, "Get off me!" Suddenly Freddie Spoon appeared. He kicked Lucas in the shins.

Lucas let go of me, and Freddie grabbed my hand shouting, "Quick! Follow me!"

He pulled me towards the fence and climbed over. But it wasn't the fence next to Mrs Next Door's garden. It was the back fence that goes into the woods, where we aren't supposed to go. But there wasn't any

time! Lucas was after me, so I shimmied
over the fence and me and Freddie Speen
escaped!

I could hear Lucas shouting, "Come back
here!" but we just ran and ran, laughing
like a pair of hysterical hyenas.

Chapter Eight

The Beast of Bramble Woods

Soon my lungs were bursting. "F-hurh Freddie Sp-rurh Spoon!" I panted.

"STOP!"

It was much darker in the woods because the trees blocked out the sky and also because it was getting quite late. We leant our backs against a tree to get our breath back. "We'll – *phewf* – wait out here a bit then – *waahf* – sneak back into the house," Freddie Spoon puffed. "Come on."

Freddie led us deeper and deeper into the woods. As we walked, he kept putting his hand in and out of his pocket, and once I thought I heard something drop into the leaves. "What have you got in your pocket?" I asked.

Freddie Spoon looked a bit shifty. Then he held out his hand. On it were some little pieces of burnt sausage all covered in fluff. "It's just … err … supplies," said Freddie Spoon. "You know, in case … err … in case we get hungry."

I pulled a face. "You're not actually going to *eat* those are you?" Freddy Spoon looked uncertain, then popped a piece of fluffy burnt sausage into his mouth. "Mmm, delicious. Want one?"

Sometimes Freddie Spoon is just too disgusting.

The woods were full of strange noises. Branches cracked beneath our feet. I asked Freddie Spoon where we were going and he said, "Don't worry, Nelly-belly. I know the way."

But after a while he
slowed down, turned
round and looked about.

I said, "What's up?"

Freddie Spoon said, "Nothing." And then he said, "Well, actually, I hate to break it to you, but I think we're lost."

I laughed. "Not really though, right?"

But Freddie Spoon put on his serious voice. He put his hand on my shoulder and said, "I'm afraid so. Completely and utterly lost. We might even have to spend the night out here. Alone."

"A-alone?" I was actually starting to get a bit scared. "You mean, with all the … the wild animals and things?"

"Oh we'll be OK," Freddie Spoon smiled. "I expect the Beast has scared most of the dangerous wild animals away."

Then I was cross. "Shut up, Freddie Spoon!" I said. "The Beast isn't here!"

"Course it's not." he smiled. "But if it was, I bet it would smell us from a mile away. It'd bite off our heads with one snap and

crunch up our bones
with its razor-sharp
teeth. There would
be nothing left of us,
only the odd severed
finger that the
Beast was too full
to swallow."

Chapter Nine
Keeping Watch

We wandered on. I held Freddie Spoon's hand. Not because I was all lovey-dovey, but just to make sure we didn't lose each other in the dark. Because it *was* dark now. Properly night-time, black as black, can't-see-more-than-a couple-of-metres dark.

Then Freddie Spoon found a
hollow tree. He said, "We can rest
in here. We must save our energy.
It could be a long
night." We
wriggled
inside,
crouched
down in
the crunchy
leaves and
took turns to
keep watch
for Lucas.

The wind swooshed
through the treetops
above us.

CREEEAKKKKK!

The branches rubbed
together around us.

Then…

CRACK!

"What was that?"
I strained to see into the darkness
but there was nothing there.

CRACK!

CRICK-CRACK!

I nearly jumped out of my skin. Freddie Spoon's voice was all trembly. "It's getting closer!" he gasped.

A knot of fear rose in my throat. And then I heard it.

I was so scared I had to cover my mouth to keep myself screaming. 'It's the Beast of Bramble Wood! It's going to bite off our heads with one snap and crunch up our bones with its razor sharp teeth. There will be nothing left of us, only the odd severed finger that the Beast is too full to swallow.' And Freddie Spoon whispered, 'Brace yourself, Nell. We're going to be tasty.'

Chapter Ten
Closer Still and Closer

The yowling got closer…

… and closer

… and closer.

Something was crashing through the trees towards us. It sounded big! I held on to Freddie Spoon as tight as tight. "Please please pleeaaasseee don't let it find us!"

Freddie Spoon said, "Be brave, Nell. Remember who we are. We're the INVINCIBLES! That means nothing can harm us."

"What are we going to do?" I whispered.

And Freddie Spoon said, "Attack is the best form of defence." Then he told me his plan.

We waited, and waited, hardly daring to breathe. The Beast got closer and closer. Suddenly Freddie Spoon shouted, "NOW!"

We jumped out of the hollow tree, screaming and yelling at the tops of our voices,

"YAAARRRGGHHHH!!!!! WE'RE INVINCIBLE!!!"

Then we leapt
right on top of it and
punched and kicked
it as hard as we could.
We showed no mercy.

"Heeelp!!"

shouted the Beast. "The
Beast of Bramble Woods
has got me!"

Chapter Eleven
We're not the Beast!

"Wait a minute!" I said. "*We're* not the
Beast! *YOU* are!"

"Don't be stupid!" said the Beast. "Do I
look like a rabid black panther?"

"Lucas?" I gasped. "Is that you?"

"Course it's me, you dodo! Now get off my head! I can't breathe!" Lucas got up, brushing leaves and mud off his trousers and pulling twigs out of his hair. His nerdy friends came out of their hiding places, brushing themselves down too.

I was relieved, but Freddie Spoon said, "If *you're* not the Beast and *we're* not the Beast then who ...or *what* ...is making that noise?"

YEEOOWWWWWLLLL!

WWWRRROOOOOWWWWLLLLL!

GRRRRAAAAAARRRRR!

Lucas gawped at him. "Err... It wasn't you trying to scare us?" Freddie Spoon slowly shook his head. And then we heard it again!

This time it was really REALLY close!
Suddenly something brushed my leg!

"ARRRGGHHHH!
It touched me! It touched me!!!"

I lunged at Lucas. Lucas grabbed me and somebody shouted,

"RUUUUUN!"

And we ran like we'd never run before.

Chapter Twelve
Don't Tell Mum

Freddie Spoon was the last one back into the garden. In fact, he was quite a way behind us, which was odd as he's almost definitely the fastest runner.

Lucas barked out orders. "Get behind the fire! It won't come near us if it sees the flames!" We huddled together, watching the fence for signs of movement, but there was nothing.

"I think we lost it!"

"That was a lucky escape!"

"*Phewee!*"

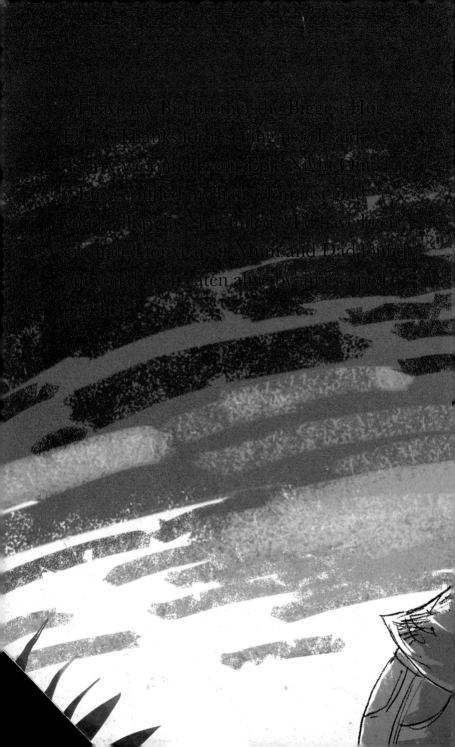

I gave my Big Brother the Biggest Hug Ever. "Thanks for rescuing us," I said. "Sorry we ruined your Epic Night Out."

Lucas ruffled my hair. "I'm just glad you're all right," he smiled. "I'd have been grounded for years if Mum and Dad found out you'd been eaten alive by an escaped panther."

I said, "I suppose we'd better tell them what's happened."

"No!" shouted everyone.

"Don't do that!" said Lucas. "They'll only get worried and make a massive fuss. You'll be safe with us. And look, we haven't finished our feast yet."

I checked the back fence one more time, then nodded. "OK then, if you're sure."

We all huddled back round the fire. It was super-cosy, all together in the dark. Lucas handed round popcorn and hot chocolate from a flask. It was delicious, and hot and sweet.

When we'd finished, Lucas wrapped me and Freddie Spoon in a blanket and we all sat watching the sparks rise up from the fire and disappear into the black night sky.

Chapter Thirteen
Mr Fluffy

Much later, Mum and Dad came out.
Mum said, "Lucas, have you seen Nell and
Freddie? They're not— Oh! *There* you are!"

Before she could ask any awkward
questions, Lucas said, "The kids just came
out to say goodnight, and I told them they
could stay for a bit."

Mum and Dad both smiled. Dad said, "Well, it's lovely to see you all playing so nicely together. Thank you, Lucas."

Seizing the moment, I said, "Does that mean that we can sleep out too?"

And Mum said, "Well, I don't see why not. You're all having such a lovely time, it would be a shame to spoil it."

I did a very small fist punch that nobody else could see. "YES!" I was so happy!

And just as I thought things couldn't get any better, along came Mr Fluffy! He licked my nose then flopped down into my lap. He was like a big fluffy hot water bottle. I stroked his silky head and then Mr Fluffy began to purr!

"YEEOOWWWWWLLLL!

WWWRROOOOOWWWWLLLLL!

GRRRRAAAAAARRRR"

Me and Lucas and William
and Joe all stared at Mr Fluffy.